For Karen, who cares
B. B.

To Frieda
K. M. D.

First edition 2011

Library of Congress Cataloging-in-Publication Data

Becker, Bonny.
The sniffles for Bear / Bonny Becker ; illustrated by Kady MacDonald Denton. —1st ed.
p. cm.
Summary: Certain that no one has even been as sick as he is,
Bear resists Mouse's efforts to cheer him and cure his cold.
ISBN 978-0-7636-4756-8
[1. Cold (Disease)—Fiction. 2. Sick—Fiction. 3. Bears—Fiction. 4. Mice—Fiction.
5. Friendship—Fiction.] I. Denton, Kady MacDonald, ill. II. Title.
PZ7.B3814Sni 2011
[E]—dc22   2010047129

11 12 13 14 15 16 SWT 10 9 8 7 6 5 4 3 2 1

Printed in Dongguan, Guangdong, China

This book was typeset in New Baskerville.
The illustrations were done in watercolor, ink, and gouache.

Candlewick Press
99 Dover Street
Somerville, Massachusetts 02144

visit us at www.candlewick.com

The Sniffles for Bear

Bonny Becker

illustrated by

Kady MacDonald Denton

CANDLEWICK PRESS

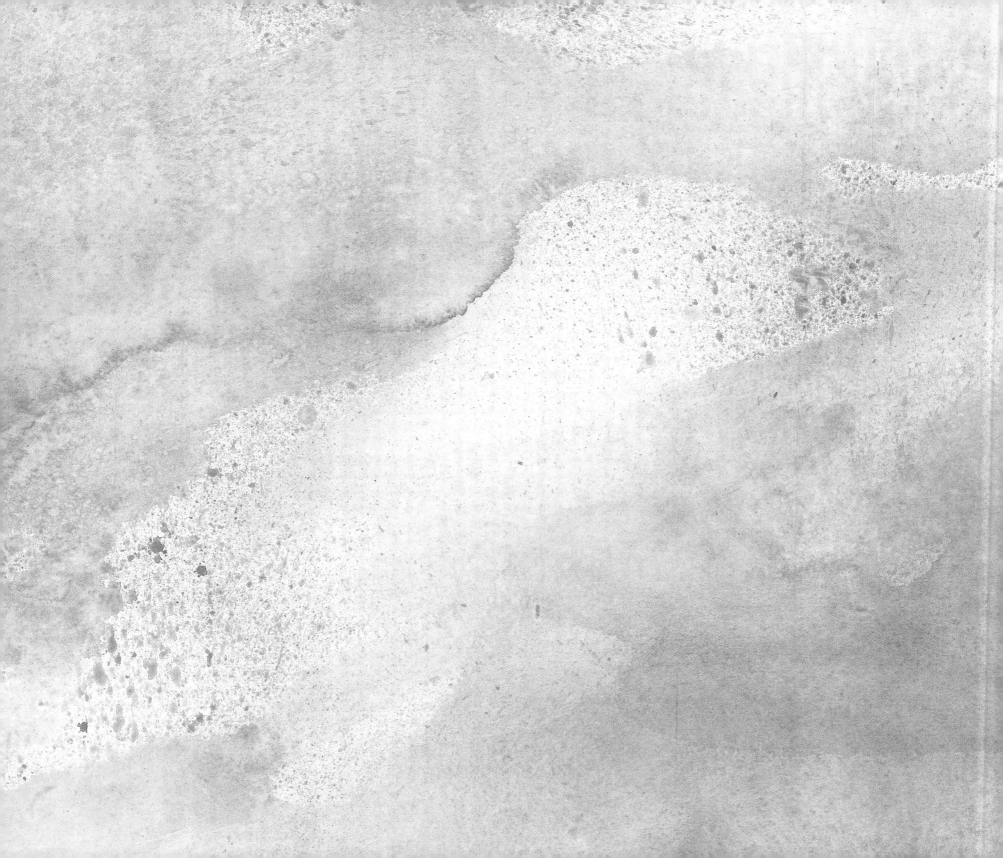

Bear was sick, very, very sick.

His eyes were red. His snout was red.

His throat was sore and gruffly.

In fact, Bear was quite sure no one

had ever been as sick as he.

One morning, Bear heard a tap, tap, tapping on his front door.

"Cub in!" he rasped.

Mouse, small and gray and bright-eyed, bustled into Bear's living room.

Bear huddled in his chair. Big and brown and sniffly-snouted.

He had a terrible cold.

"I am come!" declared Mouse. "Soon you'll be good as new!"

Bear frowned. Mouse was much too cheerful.

"I am quite ill," Bear reminded him.

"Indeed," said Mouse. "I have just the thing."

Mouse riffled through his bag, then settled next to Bear with a
yellow book in his paw.

"'It was spring,'" Mouse read. "'The sky was blue. The sun was happy.
All the birds were singing.'"

"Stop!" growled Bear. "I fear you do not appreciate the gravity of my situation."

Mouse looked sad, but his tail didn't.

"In fact, I may not be long for this world," Bear huffed.

"Oh, my," Mouse said.

"Yes," Bear murmured, coughing pitifully. "I grow weaker by the moment."

"Aah, I have just the thing," Mouse announced. "I shall soothe you with a song. *Oooooooh, she'll be coming 'round the mountain when she comes. She'll be coming 'round the mountain when she comes. She'll be coming—*"

"Disgraceful!" barked Bear.

"Don't you like singing?" asked Mouse.

"When someone is dreadfully ill, you sing mournful songs.

Everyone knows that," growled Bear. He blew his nose with a honk.

"I have just the thing," Mouse said.

He riffled through his bag.

Plunk! Plink! Plunkety, twing, twang, plonk! Mouse strummed heartily
on a tiny banjo.

"That isn't mournful at all!" cried Bear.

"It gets sad later," Mouse promised. *Twing, twang, plunk —*

"This is impossible, intolerable—" Bear started to roar, but he was too weak.

"Look!" Bear wheezed. "Look at how my paw is trembling. You must help me to my bed."

And, indeed, Mouse was most helpful.

He tucked Bear in, then whisked out
the bedroom door.

He returned balancing a big bowl
of soup on his head.
"Nettle soup," Mouse said.
"I made it myself."

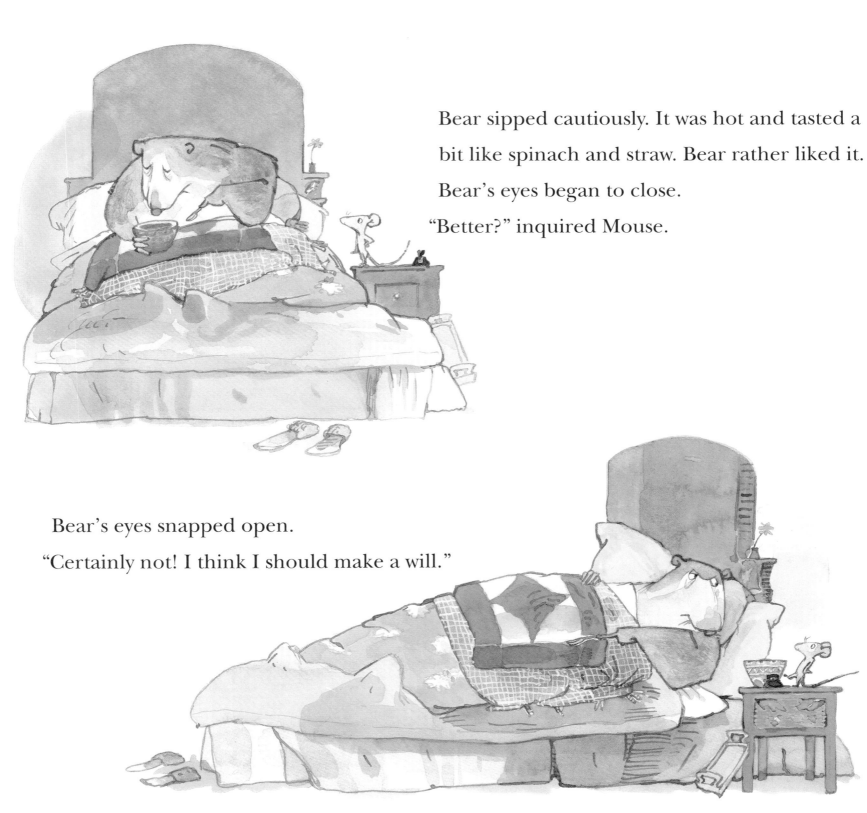

Bear sipped cautiously. It was hot and tasted a bit like spinach and straw. Bear rather liked it. Bear's eyes began to close.

"Better?" inquired Mouse.

Bear's eyes snapped open.

"Certainly not! I think I should make a will."

"Ahhhh, I have just the thing," said Mouse, fetching a pencil and little notebook from his bag.

He perched next to Bear, his pencil poised to write. Bear gazed thoughtfully at the ceiling.

"I, Bear," he said, "leave my red roller skates to . . ."

Bear paused. Mouse leaned forward eagerly.

"To Mouse," announced Bear.

"Hooray!" said Mouse.

Bear frowned. "You needn't be so happy about it.

I also leave my mop to Mouse," he added quickly.

Mouse didn't look as interested in that.

"And my wash bucket," added Bear.

At last, Mouse seemed to understand the gravity of the situation.

"Anything else?" asked Mouse.

"I'm too weak to go on," said Bear.

"Perhaps I could just add your teakettle," said Mouse helpfully.

"HAVE YOU NO DECENCY?"

bellowed Bear, sitting bolt upright in bed.

"Your strength has returned!" Mouse exclaimed.

"No, it hasn't," said Bear, falling back. "That was just the last
flicker before the dark."

"I see." Mouse folded his paws and looked very sad . . .
even his tail.

Bear's voice dropped to a whisper. "Farewell, Mouse."

"Good-bye, Bear," murmured Mouse.

Bear closed his eyes. He lay very still.

He began to snore.

After a long while, Bear opened his eyes. He saw Mouse.

"I feel better," Bear said.

Mouse nodded, but he didn't look so good. His eyes were watery, and he made sniffling sounds.

"Perhaps you better lie down," said Bear, getting out of bed.

Mouse didn't argue.

"Do you want to make a will?" Bear asked.

Mouse shook his head.

Bear carefully tucked him in. "I'm sorry you're sick," said Bear.

"Tank you, Bear," Mouse sniffled. And after a moment, he added,

"Dat was just the ting."

Bear smiled.

Mouse closed his eyes and was soon snug asleep.